THE WORLD
AND EVERYTHING IN IT

THE WORLD
AND EVERYTHING IN IT

Kevin Henkes

Greenwillow Books
An Imprint of HarperCollinsPublishers

The World and Everything in It

Copyright © 2023 by Kevin Henkes

All rights reserved. Printed in the United States of America.

For information address HarperCollins Children's Books,

a division of HarperCollins Publishers,

195 Broadway, New York, NY 10007.

www.harpercollinschildrens.com

Brown ink and watercolor paint were used to prepare the full-color art.

The text type is 30-point Tarzana Wide.

Library of Congress Cataloging-in-Publication Data

Names: Henkes, Kevin, author, illustrator.

Title: The world and everything in it / by Kevin Henkes.

Description: First edition. | New York : Greenwillow Books,

An Imprint of HarperCollinsPublishers, [2023] | Audience: Ages 4—8. |

Audience: Grades K—1. | Summary: Celebrates the big things and

little things in the world and everything in between.

Identifiers: LCCN 2022032105 | ISBN 9780063245648 (hardback) |

ISBN 9780063278752 (library binding)

Subjects: CYAC: Size—Fiction. | LCGFT: Picture books,

Classification: LCC PZ7.H389 Wp 2023 | DDC [E]—dc23

LC record available at https://lccn.loc.gov/2022032105

23 24 25 26 27 WOR 10 9 8 7 6 5 4 3 2 1

First Edition

GREENWILLOW BOOKS

For Laura, Will, and Clara

There are big things
and little things
in the world.

Little animals.

Tiny flowers.

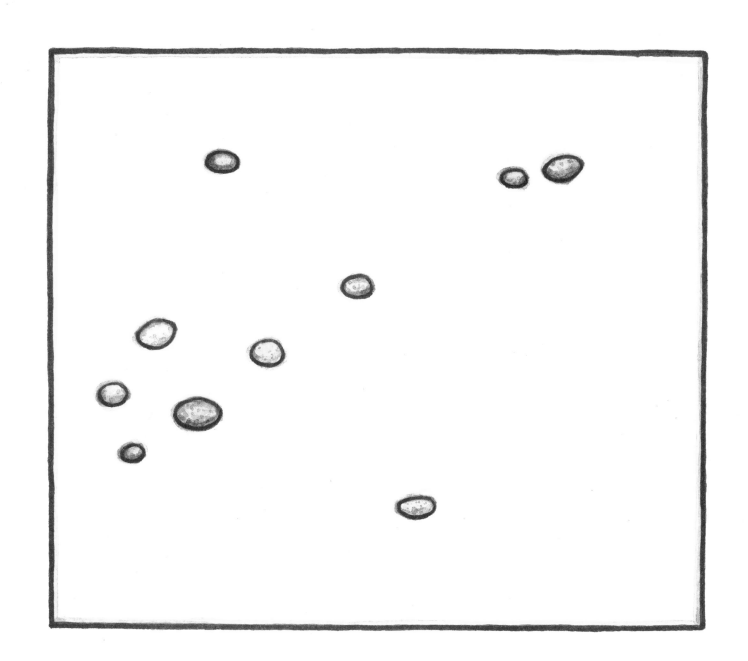

Pebbles.

Things so small
you can't see them.

The big things are big.

The sea.

The sun.

The moon.

You can have

some of the little things.

A pebble.

Or a flower.

Or a little animal.

But you can have
big things, too.

The sea is big,
but you can hold some of it
in your hands.

The sun is big,
but you can have a patch of it
on the rug on your floor.

The moon is big,
but you can see all of it
out the window in your bedroom.

There are big things
and little things
in the world.
And everything in between.

Most of the things

are in between.

Like you.

And me.

And just about anything

you can think of.

Everything is in the world.

Everything is in the world.